This book belongs to

_____

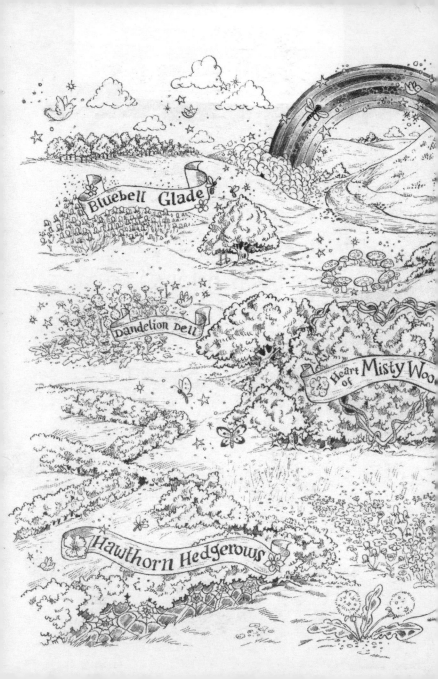

Bluebell Glade

Dandelion Dell

Heart of Misty Woo...

Hawthorn Hedgerows

Heather Hill

Sundown Hill

Crystal Cave

Golden Meadow

Moonshine Pond

Dewdrop Spring

Honeydew Meadow

Mulberry Bushes

Misty Wood Rabbit Warren

HOME
SWEET
HOME

How many **Fairy Animals** books have you collected?

 Chloe the Kitten

 Bella the Bunny

 Paddy the Puppy

 Mia the Mouse

 Hailey the Hedgehog

 Sophie the Squirrel

Poppy the Pony

And there are lots more magical adventures coming very soon!

Fairy Animals
of Misty Wood

Sophie the Squirrel

Lily Small

EGMONT

With special thanks to Gill Harvey

EGMONT
We bring stories to life

Sophie the Squirrel first published in Great Britain 2014
by Egmont UK Limited
The Yellow Building, 1 Nicholas Road, London W11 4AN

Text copyright © 2014 Hothouse Fiction Ltd
Illustrations copyright © 2014 Artful Doodlers
All rights reserved

ISBN 978 1 4052 6661 1
1 3 5 7 9 10 8 6 4 2

www.egmont.co.uk

www.hothousefiction.com

www.fairyanimals.com

A CIP catalogue record for this title is available from the British Library

Printed and bound in Great Britain by The CPI Group

54740/1

MIX
Paper
FSC FSC® C018306

EGMONT LUCKY COIN

Our story began over a century ago, when seventeen-year-old
Egmont Harald Petersen found a coin in the street.

He was on his way to buy a flyswatter, a small hand-operated
printing machine that he then set up in his tiny apartment.

The coin brought him such good luck that today Egmont has
offices in over 30 countries around the world. And that lucky
coin is still kept at the company's head offices in Denmark.

# Contents

CHAPTER ONE

Rise and Shine!

Misty Wood was brimming over with excitement. The sun was beaming happily as he stretched his rays out to every corner of the wood. The leaves on the trees were

1

rustling cheerfully. The blooms
in the meadows were bobbing
their heads joyfully in the breeze.
And everywhere you looked,
fairy animals were fluttering their
sparkling wings and whispering
behind their paws.

'Tomorrow it's the fair!' they
chattered. 'Tomorrow it's the *fair*!'

High up in an old oak tree,
a pretty little face popped out of
a hole in the trunk. The face was

RISE AND SHINE!

followed by a silky red body with sparkly violet wings. Last of all came a bushy golden tail that twitched to and fro. It was Sophie the Stardust Squirrel.

'Tomorrow is going to be the best day of my whole life!' she cried. 'I can't wait, I can't wait!' Sophie was especially excited because she and her friends were performing the opening dance at the Misty Wood fair.

4

Sophie hopped on to a branch and smoothed down her whiskers. Then she flexed her fairy wings and closed her eyes, imagining what tomorrow would be like.

The opening dance of the Misty Wood fair was always lovely. Every year, some clever Bark Badgers made a wooden totem pole, carved with woodland scenes and beautiful, swirling patterns. It was placed in the middle of a

big grassy clearing, then brightly

coloured strands of flowers were

attached like ribbons, to stream

down from the top. Each of the

dancers held on to one of the

strands as they skipped round

the pole.

Today, the pole would finally

be ready and Sophie and her

friends would get the chance to

have one last practice.

Sophie jiggled her tail at the

very thought, and scampered
down the old oak tree. She was
so excited, she couldn't stay still!
When she reached the bottom, she
jumped back up again, imagining
that the tree was the pole. As she
twisted and turned round the
gnarled trunk she thought of all
the other fairy animals, cheering
loudly as she and her friends
performed the dance.

Just as she reached the top of

the tree, she heard someone

shouting.

'What's all that scraping and

scuffling?' Sophie's mum called.

Sophie peered down through

8

the branches. Her mum was poking her head out of the nest in the cosy hollow where they lived, looking this way and that.

'It's only me, Mum,' Sophie replied.

'Sophie! Whatever are you up to?' asked her mum, looking up at her. 'You're making so much noise you woke Sammy from his nap.'

'Oh, I'm sorry, Mum!' Sophie exclaimed. Sammy was Sophie's

little brother. He was still very young so he always had a mid-day snooze. 'I didn't mean to wake him. I'm just so excited about dancing tomorrow.'

Sophie's mum smiled. 'Yes, I understand. I remember dancing at the fair when I was your age. It was so much fun. But try not to get *too* excited, Sophie – look at what you've done to our tree!'

'Done? I haven't done

anything . . .' Sophie began. But as she looked around the branches, she clapped her paw to her mouth. The old oak tree was shimmering silver from top to toe! The leaves were no longer green. The trunk was no longer brown. Every single part of the tree was covered in stardust!

Like all of the other fairy animals in Misty Wood, Stardust Squirrels had their own special job.

Their big, bushy tails sprinkled stardust whenever the squirrels gave them a shake. They were supposed to scatter the dust lightly over Misty Wood so that it twinkled gently. But the oak tree wasn't just twinkling now. It was *glowing*!

'Never mind,' chuckled Sophie's mum. 'The next time it rains it will all get washed away. And, in the meantime, it's quite

nice having the brightest tree in the whole wood – at least we'll be able to find our way home in the dark! Now, it's time you went to your practice.'

'Oh! Is it?' Sophie sat up on her back legs and wiggled her whiskers.

Sophie's mum nodded.

'Hurrah, hurray!' cheered Sophie. 'We're going to dance around the totem pole at last!'

13

With two enormous flicks of her tail she bounded down the tree, scattering more stardust. She looked up at her mum to wave goodbye. 'Uh-oh . . .' she murmured.

Her mum's head had turned silver now too. It was hard to tell where she ended and the tree began!

Sophie's mum laughed and gave her head a shake, sending

a cloud of stardust shimmering to the ground. 'Good luck,' she called. 'And mind what you do with that tail!'

'I will,' Sophie said with a grin. 'See you later, Mum.' And with a flutter of her fairy wings, she flew off to find her friends.

CHAPTER TWO

Practice Makes Perfect

Sophie rose up above the trees, enjoying the feel of the breeze ruffling her soft fur. First of all she had to fetch her friend Katie from Hawthorn Hedgerows.

It was a beautiful sunny day, and the delicious scent of hawthorn blossom wafted towards Sophie as she swooped over the hedges. Soon, the glint of a shiny dewdrop caught her eye, and she dived down to land near a silvery cobweb.

'Katie!' she called. 'Where are you?'

'I'm over here!' a tinkly voice meowed.

Sophie peeped over the cobweb and spotted her friend's tabby fur and silvery wings. Katie was a Cobweb Kitten. It was the Cobweb Kittens' job to collect dewdrops every morning from Dewdrop Spring, then use them to decorate the cobwebs in Misty Wood.

Sophie watched as Katie fished a dewdrop from her little basket and balanced it perfectly on one of the cobweb's delicate threads.

'Almost finished!' said Katie.

'Only two more to go!'

'Good,' said Sophie. 'It's time for our final dance practice.'

'I know,' Katie purred. 'I was so excited this morning, I kept dropping my dewdrops! That's why I haven't quite finished yet.'

'I can help you,' Sophie offered. 'Shall we place one each?'

Katie gave a big smile. 'Yes please!' She pointed a snowy-white paw to the top of a nearby hedge.

'Could you put one on that tiny cobweb over there?'

Sophie nodded eagerly. Then she bounded forwards and scooped a dewdrop from Katie's basket. It glimmered like a precious diamond in her paws. Holding it carefully, she carried it over to the cobweb. She felt honoured to be helping Katie do her job. Sophie placed the dewdrop on the silky strand of web and hopped back.

'Ooh, thank you, Sophie –
that looks lovely,' Katie said.

Sophie turned to Katie and
smiled. 'Come on then, let's go
and get Bonnie.'

The two friends fluttered off
towards Honeydew Meadow.
Bonnie was a Bud Bunny. The
Bud Bunnies' special job was to
nudge the flower buds into bloom
by twitching their noses against
them. Now, thanks to their hard

work, the meadow was bursting with all the colours of the rainbow.

Sophie and Katie hovered over the sea of colour for a moment, looking for their friend. In the middle of a patch of pale blue flowers, Sophie spotted Bonnie's sparkly pink wings and soft white fur.

'There she is!' Sophie cried. 'She's just about to open another flower.'

Bonnie was sitting perfectly
still, with her nose very close to
a nodding flower bud. As Sophie
and Katie watched, Bonnie's
nose twitched . . . and one by one,

the petals of the flower burst open.

Sophie and Katie flew down to land beside Bonnie, clapping their paws. Bonnie's long white ears pricked up at the sight of her two friends.

'Hi, Bonnie! Your flowers are so pretty,' Sophie said. 'Are you ready to come to the dance practice?'

Bonnie twirled her whiskers. 'Ooh, is it time?' she asked.

Sophie and Katie nodded.

'I'd better just tell my mum. She's working over there,' said Bonnie, waving her paw in the direction of some brightly coloured tulips.

Bonnie's mum was sitting in the middle of the tulips, twitching her nose against the glossy buds. The friends scampered up to her just as one of the tulips burst into bloom. Its petals were as yellow

and shiny as the sun.

'Mum, can I go to my dance practice?' Bonnie asked.

'Of course.' Bonnie's mum smiled at the little fairy animals and her fluffy cotton tail began thumping on the ground. 'I have a nice surprise for you, too.'

'Ooh, I love surprises!' Sophie exclaimed and her tail twitched, sending a puff of stardust into the air.

'What kind of surprise is it?' Bonnie asked, hopping about to catch some stardust on the tips of her ears.

Bonnie's mum smoothed back her whiskers and leaned towards them. 'I'm going to make each of you a flower garland to wear when you do your dance at the fair,' she said. 'I'm going to use the prettiest flowers in all of Misty Wood's meadows!'

Sophie was so pleased, her wings started fluttering. As she rose into the air her tail twitched this way and that, showering stardust all over the tulips.

'Thank you!' she cried.

'Thank you!' Bonnie and Katie chorused.

'You're welcome,' Bonnie's mum said with a smile.

'Now, we just have to go and get Polly,' Sophie said.

'Have fun!' Bonnie's mum called as she hopped over to a big cluster of crimson poppy buds and began nudging them open.

Sophie, Katie and Bonnie swooped away, heading towards Dandelion Dell. It wasn't very far, and soon they could see golden dandelions spread out like a carpet of sunshine below them.

The Pollen Puppies were hard at work, bouncing from one patch

of blooms to another, wagging their tails as they went. They were doing a very important job – with each wag of their tails they spread pollen, so that there would be even more dandelions next year.

The three friends fluttered round in circles, looking for Polly.

'There she is!' cried Sophie, with a beat of her violet wings. 'Down there, playing with Paddy.'

They floated down closer.

As usual, the Pollen Puppies weren't *just* working. They were having lots of fun, chasing each other through the dell, batting each other with their fluffy paws and yelping with excitement. Polly and Paddy were racing down rows of dandelions, their floppy ears flying.

'Polly!' called Katie, fluttering down to land. 'It's time for our last dance practice.'

Polly skidded to a halt next to

a tall, tufty dandelion. 'Oh!' she cried. 'Is it really?' She clapped her paws, and her coppery brown tail wagged harder than ever.

Sophie, Katie and Bonnie gathered round.

'Sorry, Paddy,' said Polly. 'I have to go now. Do you think you can finish off on your own?'

'Of course!' Paddy panted, his little pink tongue hanging out. 'But first I'm going to race my tail.'

35

'How do you race your own tail?' Sophie asked with a frown.

'Easy peasy,' Paddy replied. 'Look!' And with that, he bounded off, his tail wagging so fast it became a golden blur.

Polly smoothed down her ears and rustled her golden wings. 'I'm ready,' she told the others. 'Let's go!'

Sophie, Katie, Bonnie and Polly flew off across the dell and into the Heart of Misty Wood. As they soared through the trees Sophie's wings flapped faster and faster – she couldn't wait to see the totem pole. But when they got to the clearing where the dance was supposed to be taking place, there

was no pole to be seen.

They fluttered down to the ground and looked about. An old Bark Badger with silvery wings was busy carving beautiful patterns into the bark of a nearby tree.

'Excuse me,' Sophie said, scampering over to him. 'Do you know where the totem pole is? We've been chosen to perform the opening dance at the fair tomorrow and we need to practise.'

The badger stopped what he was doing and smiled at Sophie. 'I'm sorry, little Stardust Squirrel, but the pole isn't quite ready yet,' he said. 'My badger friends are poorly so I am decorating it all on my own. It won't be ready until the morning.'

'But the fair starts in the morning!' Sophie gasped.

The four friends looked at each other. They had worked out

39

all their steps. They'd gone through them so many times that they knew them by heart. But they'd never practised with ribbons and a pole. What were they going to do?

CHAPTER THREE

Hello, Mr Bluebird!

Sophie rubbed her nose with her paw. 'We'll have to find a different kind of pole,' she said, 'and pretend that it's the proper one.'

'Yes,' Katie agreed. 'There

has to be something that will do, somewhere in Misty Wood.'

They sat in a huddle and tried to think. What would be tall and strong and ribbony enough to make a good practice pole? They scratched their heads and they tugged their whiskers. But it was no use – they couldn't think of anything.

'Maybe we should just go and look for one,' Sophie said at last.

'Yes,' said Bonnie. 'But we'll have to be quick. We'll never be ready by tomorrow if we don't find one soon!'

They unfurled their wings and flew off together to begin the hunt. They soared over Hawthorn Hedgerows, but there were only twigs and bushes there. Then they made for Honeydew Meadow, but they could only see pretty flowers.

Next, they glided around the

Heart of Misty Wood, but the trees there were too tall and tangly. When they flew over Moonshine Pond they saw lots of dragonflies, but they didn't see anything that looked like a good practice pole.

'What are we going to *do*?' wailed Katie, her tabby tail drooping.

'Let's try Dewdrop Spring,' Sophie said.

'But that's just water,' said

44

Katie sadly. 'I've never seen anything like a pole there.'

Sophie knew that her friend was probably right. But they couldn't give up – not until they had searched the whole of Misty Wood. As they fluttered towards Dewdrop Spring, Sophie spotted something in the distance that made her heart leap.

'Look!' she exclaimed, pointing down. 'It's perfect!'

There, on the bank of the
spring, stood an elegant willow
tree. Its trunk was tall and straight,
but its thin branches swept down
all around it – just like ribbons.

'Oh, yes, of course,' purred
Katie happily. 'Well done, Sophie!'

'Hurray!' cried Bonnie.

Polly yapped gleefully and
did a loop-the-loop, then zoomed
down to the willow tree at full
speed. Giggling and chattering,

HELLO, MR BLUEBIRD!

47

the other three followed her. They skipped round the tree, deciding which branches would make the best ribbons.

Suddenly, they heard a voice.

'What's all that noise around my tree?' it twittered.

The four friends fell silent at once. They squinted up into the willow tree.

'It's only . . . only . . . us . . .' Sophie began, peering through

48

the branches. She couldn't see

anything at first, but then, right at

the top of the tree, she spied a little

nest. And perched on the nest was

a bluebird, with feathers the colour

of a bright summer sky.

'We're sorry, Mr Bluebird,'
Sophie said. 'It's the Misty
Wood fair tomorrow, and we're
performing the opening dance
– but we don't have a pole to
practise with. Your tree is the only
thing we've found. Would you
mind if we use it, just for a little
while?'

The bluebird hopped out of his
nest and flew down to the ground.

'The opening dance, eh?' he chirped, tilting his head.

'Yes,' Sophie nodded.

'That sounds very important,' tweeted the bluebird. 'Important enough for you to use my tree. But won't you need some music to dance to?'

'Oh, yes,' said Bonnie. 'We'll have music tomorrow. The Moss Mouse band will be playing for us while we dance.'

'But what about now?' asked the bluebird. 'How are you going to practise if you don't have any music *now*?'

Sophie, Katie, Bonnie and Polly looked at each other. The bluebird was right. They couldn't *really* know how the dance would go if they'd never tried it with music.

'Well . . .' said Sophie slowly, twitching her whiskers. She was beginning to feel a bit nervous.

'I suppose we'll just have to hope for the best.'

'No, no, no,' chirruped the bluebird, shaking his head. 'That won't do at all. You *must* practise with music. And I know exactly what music you should have.'

'You do?' Polly looked at him hopefully and her tail began to wag.

'It just so happens that I'm one of the best singers in the whole of Misty Wood,' said the bluebird

53

proudly. 'So, as you've come to *my* tree, and want to dance under *my* nest, I think I should help you out.'

'Really?' Sophie gasped. 'You'll sing for us?'

The bluebird puffed out his feathery chest. 'I certainly will. Are you ready?'

Fumbling in excitement, the friends scampered around the tree, quickly deciding on which willow branches to use. When each of

them was holding a branch, the bluebird spread his wings, threw back his head and began to sing in a sweet, soaring voice.

It was the most beautiful song that any of them had ever heard. They danced in time, weaving in and out of each other round the tree. First one way, then another, and then . . .

'Ow!' cried Sophie, stopping with a bump.

The bluebird stopped singing and flew over to her. 'What is it, little squirrel?' he asked.

'It's my tail,' gasped Sophie. 'I can't move it!'

Sophie's friends gathered round.

'It's all tangled up in the branches,' Katie meowed.

Sophie pulled her tail one way. Then she pulled it the other way. But it was no use. She was well and truly stuck!

CHAPTER FOUR

Triple Trouble

'Oh, no!' Sophie cried. 'How can we practise for the dance if I'm stuck to the tree?' She looked at her friends and her brown eyes widened in fear. 'What if I'm

stuck here forever?'

'Don't worry.' Bonnie hopped over and patted Sophie with her paw. 'We'll soon sort it out.'

'We just need to be patient,' Katie agreed. 'We'll untangle it one branch at a time.'

'I'll sing you a patient song, if you like,' the little bluebird chirped, perching himself on a branch in front of Sophie. He began tweeting very slowly and gently.

Polly, Bonny and Katie began working on Sophie's tail. Slowly and gently, in time with the song, they untwisted the long, thin willow branches one by one. Sophie watched them anxiously over her shoulder. Sometimes they accidentally pulled her fur, and she had to try hard not to yelp. To take her mind off it she closed her eyes and thought of yummy acorns instead.

Just as Sophie was thinking
of her twenty-second acorn, Polly
clapped her paws.

'You're free!' she woofed.

Sophie opened her eyes. The
bluebird was flying round and
round in a circle, chirping wildly.

Sophie hopped forwards. It felt so good to be able to move again. 'Thank you!' she exclaimed in relief. 'And don't worry, I'll be doubly careful with my tail from now on!'

They all took their positions around the tree, and the bluebird flew up to the top.

'All ready?' he called down.

'Yes!' they chorused.

He opened his little beak and

began his beautiful song again. The dance started, and soon Sophie had forgotten all about trapping her tail. As she and her friends skipped in time with the bluebird's melody she felt herself getting more and more excited.

Tomorrow is going to be so wonderful, Sophie thought to herself. *It's going to be the best day of my . . .*

'*Ahhhhh-TCHOOO!*'

Sophie jumped as a loud sneeze rang out across the banks of the spring. Then it got even worse. '*Ahhhhh-TCHOOO! Cough, cough, COUGH!*' she heard.

Sophie stopped dancing and looked round. Bonnie was doubled over behind her. Her floppy ears were lying flat and her pink eyes were streaming.

'Oh, no!' gulped Sophie.

She could see at once what the

problem was. Bonnie's normally snowy white fur was glimmering silver. Sophie had got so excited while she'd been dancing that she'd showered Bonnie in stardust!

'*Cough cough cough*,' spluttered Bonnie. 'I've got stardust up my – *ahhh-tchooo* – nose.'

'I'm so sorry,' cried Sophie. 'Oh dear, my tail's causing all sorts of problems today.'

Polly let go of her branch and

bounded over. 'Don't worry,' she yapped. 'I'll soon fix it.'

She scampered around Bonnie, wagging her tail, just as she did when she was flicking pollen in the meadows. *Flick flick flick*, went her tail. *Flick flick flickety flick* . . .

Bonnie started to giggle. 'It tickles!' she cried, as Polly's tail flicked away at her fur.

The bluebird flew above them,

66

TRIPLE TROUBLE

chirping jauntily, and soon Polly
had flicked all the stardust away.

'Oh, well done, Polly!' Sophie
exclaimed. 'You've done a brilliant
job!'

'Yes, thanks Polly,' agreed
Bonnie, wiping her eyes dry. 'I'm
ready to start dancing again.'

'Right,' said Sophie. 'And
this time my tail won't cause any
problems. I won't let it!'

So off round the tree they

went. Sophie concentrated really hard. She mustn't shake her tail too much and she mustn't get it stuck.

'I'll tuck it between my legs,' she muttered to herself.

As the practice went on, Sophie began to feel more happy and confident. With her tail tucked tightly between her legs, there were no more problems. But just as they whirled round the tree one last time,

Sophie suddenly felt herself hurtling forwards.

'Wahhhhhh!' she cried.

THUMP. She fell flat on her face.

'Help!' squeaked Bonnie, bumping into Sophie.

'Uh-oh!' yelped Polly, landing on Bonnie's back.

'Oh, no!' meowed Katie, falling head-over-heels on top of them all!

'Oh no, oh no, oh no!' the

bluebird tweeted, as he hovered above.

The four fairy animals lay in a heap on the ground, their paws, wings and tails in a higgledy-

piggledy jumble. Sophie lay at the bottom of the pile, trying to work out what had happened. And then she realised. She'd tucked her tail so tightly between her legs that she'd tripped right over it!

A big fat tear rolled down Sophie's cheek. 'It's all my fault,' she wept. 'Everything's going wrong and I'll never be able to get the dance right. *Never!*'

CHAPTER FIVE

Shooting Star!

A delicious smell wafted through
the cosy hollow in the old oak tree.
It was Sophie's favourite dinner
– acorn soup – and her dad had
just finished making it. But Sophie

didn't feel at all hungry. Her
baby brother banged his wooden
spoon and gurgled impatiently,
but Sophie was quite sure that
she wouldn't be able to eat even
the tiniest bit. She sat on her little
sycamore stool in the corner,
feeling glum.

'What's the matter?' Sophie's
mum asked. 'Didn't your practice
go well?'

Sophie shook her head. 'No,

it didn't.' She could feel her lip beginning to wobble.

'Oh, never mind,' her dad said with a smile. 'It can't have been that bad.'

'But it *was*,' Sophie cried. 'Everyone's going to laugh at me at the fair. I can't dance at all!'

'Yes you can,' said her dad. 'You're a lovely dancer.'

'Not any more,' Sophie said, her head drooping low.

Sophie's mum hopped over and stroked her silky fur. 'What happened?'

'My tail spoiled everything,' Sophie muttered. 'First I got it stuck. Then it showered stardust all over Bonnie and made her cough and sneeze. And then I tripped over it – and everyone else tripped over me! Stupid tail!'

'Oh, dear,' said Sophie's mum. She wrapped her own bushy tail

round Sophie in a big hug. 'But try not to get too upset. Things always go wrong in rehearsals – I'm sure it will be fine at the fair.'

Normally, her mum's hugs made Sophie feel a lot better. But not today. All she could think about was how terrible the dance was going to be. She started to cry, and buried her face in her paws.

'It's going . . . to be . . . awful,' she sobbed.

'Now, don't you worry,' her
dad said, giving her one of his
twinkly eyed smiles. 'I think I have
an idea.'

'You have?' Sophie peeked at

him hopefully through her paws.

Sophie's dad whispered in her mum's ear, and her mum nodded, her eyes sparkling.

'Oh, yes,' her mum said in a mysterious voice. 'That will work. Definitely!'

Sophie's dad winked at Sophie and beckoned to her. 'Come on,' he said. 'You and I are going out.'

'What . . . *now*?' It was dark outside, and Sophie hardly ever

went out at night.

Her dad nodded and held out his paw. 'Follow me,' he said.

Sophie felt a tiny bit nervous at first, going out in the dark, but she knew she was safe with her dad. He opened his strong red wings and led her up, up, up towards the glowing, pearly face of the moon. Soon they were high above the treetops, with nothing but twinkling stars around them.

Sophie looked down and gasped. Misty Wood lay out like a map below her – it looked very beautiful in the moonlight. There were the flower buds in the meadows, drooping their little heads as they slept. There were the shimmering waters of Dewdrop Spring. Then Sophie saw flashes of pale light, and pointed down excitedly.

'Look, Dad!' she cried.

The Moonbeam Moles were flitting through the darkness below them like shadows, catching glowing moonbeams to drop into Moonshine Pond. Sophie's dad nodded, then he carried on flying upwards. Sophie had to flap her wings very hard to be able to keep up.

'Why are we going so high?' she panted.

Her dad looked back at her

and smiled. 'It's just a little bit further.'

Sophie fluttered up next to him, panting from all the effort.

'This is what we've come for,' her dad explained. 'Look. Up there.'

Sophie looked. Above her head, the most beautiful shooting star flew past, leaving a rainbow-coloured trail of stardust behind it.

'Wow!' Sophie breathed.

'Now, be quick,' her dad said.

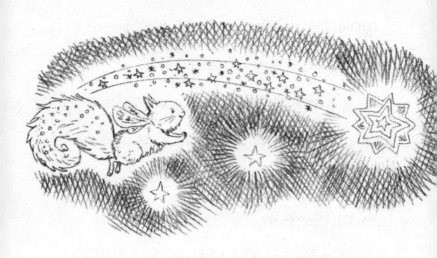

'Fly after it and catch some of that stardust in your tail.'

Sophie twitched her bushy tail excitedly. All of a sudden she didn't feel tired at all. The star was the

most lovely thing she'd ever seen!
She whooshed after it.

The star danced across the
sky, making wonderful patterns as
it went. Sometimes it zig-zagged,
or soared in spiralling circles.
Sometimes it even made the shape
of flower petals as it looped round
the shining moon.

As Sophie chased the star,
she twisted her tail this way and
that to catch as much stardust as

she could. She completely forgot
all her worries about the dance
practice. She even forgot about
the fair. All she could think about
was how happy she was to be
out catching rainbow-coloured
stardust in her fluffy tail.

The shooting star did one
last enormous loop, then it
disappeared behind the moon.
Sophie gazed after it. Had it really
gone? She felt a bit sad. Her dad

flew up and placed his paw on her shoulder.

'Shooting stars never last long,' he said, 'and you did very well to catch so much stardust. You see, the dust from a shooting star is special.'

'Really?' Sophie's eyes shone.

'Yes.' Her dad smiled. 'It is magical, and now that the shooting stardust is in your tail you'll be able to get it to behave perfectly in

the dance tomorrow.'

Sophie twitched her ears in disbelief. 'Truly?'

'Really and truly.' Her dad nodded solemnly. 'As long as you believe in the magic . . .'

CHAPTER SIX

The Big Day

Dawn was breaking over Misty Wood, spreading its pale golden light across the hedgerows and hills, meadows and valleys.

Sophie opened her eyes. She

gazed up at the cluster of oak leaves that dangled over her mossy bed, and frowned. A strange memory was taking shape in her head – or had it been a dream? Something about chasing a shooting star . . .

Sophie hopped out of bed and gave her tail a little shake. A puff of rainbow-coloured stardust filled the air, and drifted down on to her soft pillow. Sophie gasped.

It hadn't been a dream at all!

Sophie scampered across the

cosy hollow to join her mum, dad

and Sammy at their breakfast table made from polished conkers.

'Good morning, Sophie,' said her mum. 'Come and have some porridge. You're going to need plenty of energy today!'

Sophie sat down and took a mouthful of porridge. She knew her mum was right, but she was starting to feel nervous. Was her dad right about the shooting stardust? Would her tail really be OK?

Sophie had eaten half her porridge when she heard excited chatter coming from outside.

'Sophie, are you ready?' she heard Polly yap.

'It's time to go,' Katie meowed.

'It's almost time for the fair!' Bonnie called.

Sophie leaped up from the table, her tail twitching. A cloud of the special stardust shimmered into the bowls of porridge, like

93

rainbow-coloured sugar.

'Whoops!' Sophie exclaimed.

'Yay!' Sammy cried, looking at the porridge with glee.

'Good luck,' Sophie's dad said, as Bonnie, Katie and Polly's noses peeped into the hollow. 'We'll see you there. And don't forget what I told you!' he added with a wink at Sophie.

'I won't,' promised Sophie. She took a deep breath and headed out

94

to join her friends.

Buzzing with energy, the four friends spread their wings and flew out between the trees. It was still early, but lots of fairy animals were already busy, bustling about making preparations for the fair.

Sophie spotted Old Frannie the Fern Fox's tent, draped in garlands of copper beech leaves, where she would sit telling fairy fortunes all day. Just beyond,

Sophie saw the Misty Wood bees hard at work, building their fairground honeycomb maze. Sophie loved wandering around in the maze, giggling with her friends as they got lost in its endless twists and turns.

As they got closer to the Heart of Misty Wood, Katie pointed at the shimmering, swaying cobweb marquee, made from the silky threads of hundreds of Misty Wood

spiders. Inside the marquee would be all sorts of stalls displaying the fairy animals' favourite treats.

Every year there was a *Guess How Many Blackberries* competition. There would be a cake stall laden with mounds of hazelnut cakes and honey buns, acorn pies and conker crunchies. Flowers from the meadows would brighten every corner and, once the Cobweb Kittens had got to work,

the whole marquee would be glistening with dewdrops from Dewdrop Spring!

Sophie couldn't wait for the fair to begin. It was all going to be such fun!

They flew onwards towards the clearing where the grand opening was to take place. Sophie remembered that, before they could explore any of the treats that the fair had in store, they had to

perform their dance. She started feeling a little nervous again . . .

Down below, in the clearing, Sophie could see some Bark Badgers. They were gathered in a huddle, their silvery wings folded neatly over their stripy black and white backs. They seemed to be having some kind of meeting. Sophie suddenly felt worried. She couldn't see the totem pole anywhere. Shouldn't the badgers

have put it in place by now?

Sophie and her friends fluttered down and scampered over to the badgers. 'We're here!' Sophie cried. 'We're ready to do our opening dance.'

The badgers turned to them, their faces sad. Sophie's heart thudded. Now she knew for sure that something was wrong.

'Where's the totem pole?' she asked.

The badgers parted, so that the four friends could see what they had been gathered round. There, on the vivid green grass, lay the totem pole covered in amazing carvings, with ribbons of flowers streaming from one end. Sophie's eyes shone when she saw how beautiful it was.

But then she noticed something. There was a problem. A *big* problem. The pole was broken in

SOPHIE THE SQUIRREL

two, right in the middle.

'We just finished decorating it, but it was so heavy and we dropped it,' explained the badger they had met yesterday. He gave a long, sad sigh. 'We're very, very sorry.'

Sophie couldn't believe it. She blinked hard, hoping she might see something different when she opened her eyes – but the totem pole was still broken.

'So . . . what shall we do now?' she asked in a very small voice.

'Well . . .' the badger stroked his chin and shuffled from one paw to the other. He looked very upset. 'I'm afraid that there's nothing we can do. I'm very sorry, but the dance will just have to be cancelled.'

CHAPTER SEVEN

Rainbow Bright!

Cancelled! Sophie rubbed her ears with her paws, hoping she had misheard.

The sun was peeping through the trees around the clearing, and

crowds of fairy animals had started to arrive. Over to one side, the Moss Mouse band had begun to play. There was no time left.

A tear rolled down Sophie's cheek. She sat down next to Polly, Bonnie and Katie. They were all too sad to say anything. The other fairy animals who had begun to gather to watch the dance looked at them curiously.

Sophie thought about how

wonderful everything had seemed last night, flying high in the dark sky, chasing the shooting star. She thought of practising around the willow tree and how her dad had promised that the magical rainbow stardust would make her tail behave. None of that mattered any more.

But, as Sophie remembered all that had happened the day before, an idea began to form in her mind.

She scrubbed her tears away and leaped to her feet.

'I know what we're going to do!' she called. 'Everyone follow me!'

Polly, Bonnie and Katie's eyes widened, and they jumped up excitedly.

'Where are we going?' asked
Katie.

'You'll soon find out,' said
Sophie. 'Come on, everyone!'
she called to all the other fairy
animals.

Sophie set off, half-scampering,

half-fluttering, checking over
her shoulder that everyone was
following. Around the honeycomb
maze, past the cobweb marquee
– she hurried on until she reached
the banks of Dewdrop Spring.

The willow tree stood there,
its branches draping down to the
ground. Sophie bounded up to it.
She gave a shake of her tail, and
a little cloud of rainbow-coloured
stardust puffed out. Then she flew

up and around the tree, shaking her tail until the whole willow glittered with glorious colours. Soon its trunk glowed red, orange and yellow, and its branches looked like green, purple, pink and blue ribbons – only even prettier!

'Wow!' gasped Katie, Bonnie and Polly, as Sophie landed beside them.

'How did you do that?' Polly woofed, her tail wagging wildly.

113

'It looks *beautiful*!'

'It's magic,' Sophie said with a grin.

The fairy animals that had followed them began to flutter about, chattering to each other and spreading the news: the dance was back on! The Bark Badgers looked very relieved indeed.

As the crowd began to grow, the band arrived and took their places next to the tree. Just then,

Bonnie's mum appeared. Her paws were full with the flower garlands that she'd promised.

'Here you are!' she cried. 'You can't dance without your garlands!'

She slipped one over Bonnie's head. It was made of golden buttercups and soft blue harebells, fluffy meadowsweet and bright red poppies. It looked beautiful next to the rainbow colours of the willow

tree. The crowd cheered and clapped as Sophie, Katie and Polly put their garlands on too.

Sophie's mum arrived and flew over to give her a big, soft hug with her bushy tail. The she joined Sophie's dad and Sammy, right

at the front. They were all waving excitedly. Sophie thought she might burst with pride!

When all of the animals had gathered on the banks of the spring, the band played a fanfare with their lily trumpets. Sophie, Bonnie, Polly and Katie carefully took hold of the branches they'd practised with the day before.

Just as they were about to begin, Sophie looked up and saw

the bluebird on his branch. But he wasn't blue any more. Just like the tree, his feathers were now every colour of the rainbow!

Oops, thought Sophie. But the bluebird didn't seem to mind at all. He puffed up his colourful chest proudly and began trilling his beautiful song, in harmony with the band.

Sophie took a deep breath. *Tail, behave!* she said in her head.

She hoped the shooting stardust would work.

Sophie's heart soared as she skipped round the tree, first this way, then that. Her tail didn't shake, so nobody sneezed. And it stayed in position, so it didn't get tangled up in the branches or trip her up. She was surrounded by a blur of lovely colours as the branches of the willow tree swished to and fro. It reminded her of the

beautiful shooting star, and how it had drawn patterns so gracefully across the sky.

The crowd clapped and cheered as the four friends danced faster and faster round the tree. Sophie caught a glimpse of her mum and dad smiling, and her little brother laughing and clapping his paws in time.

And then, all at once, it was over. The whole of Misty

RAINBOW BRIGHT!

Wood cheered and clapped and drummed the ground with their paws. Sophie thought they might never stop!

At last the clapping began to die down, and the fairy animals set off to explore all the exciting things on offer at the fair. Sophie rushed over to her mum and dad to give them both a huge hug.

'We did it!' she squealed.

'You were fantastic!' her dad

grinned. 'My little star!'

Sophie laughed. 'Oh, but it was the *shooting* star that helped me!' she exclaimed, and gave her tail a little shake. She gasped. There was no rainbow-coloured stardust left. Instead, a cloud of the usual silvery stardust shimmered in the air, then floated gently to the ground.

'It's all gone!' Sophie stared at her dad. 'I haven't shaken my

tail since decorating the tree. I must have used it all up before the dance!' Sophie frowned. 'But how did I manage to get my tail to behave if I didn't have any magical stardust left?'

Her dad patted her head with his paw. 'Sometimes, all you need is to believe,' he said with a smile. 'You believed the stardust was going to help you – and it did. It gave you the confidence you

needed to do the dance perfectly.
Now you can believe in yourself!'

'Wow – that really is magic!'
Sophie gasped.

'Yes, it is,' said her dad. 'Now,
it's time you and your friends went
off to enjoy the fair. You deserve it
after all that hard work.'

Sophie had been thinking so
much about the dance she'd
almost forgotten that a whole day
of wonderful treats and surprises

lay ahead. As she fluttered off to join Katie, Bonnie and Polly, she saw someone else flying along beside her.

'Can I come too?' chirped the bluebird. 'I want to show off my new colourful feathers.'

'Of course you can!' Sophie exclaimed.

Together, Sophie and her friends flew off towards the cobweb marquee. The bluebird tweeted a

RAINBOW BRIGHT!

cheerful tune as they went and Sophie hummed along. She swished her tail happily and a trail of silver stardust shimmered in the sky behind them. What an exciting morning it had been! Today really *was* turning into the very best day of her life!

Turn the page for some fun Misty Wood activities!

Help Sophie find the acorn cup of delicious honey at the centre of the maze.

START

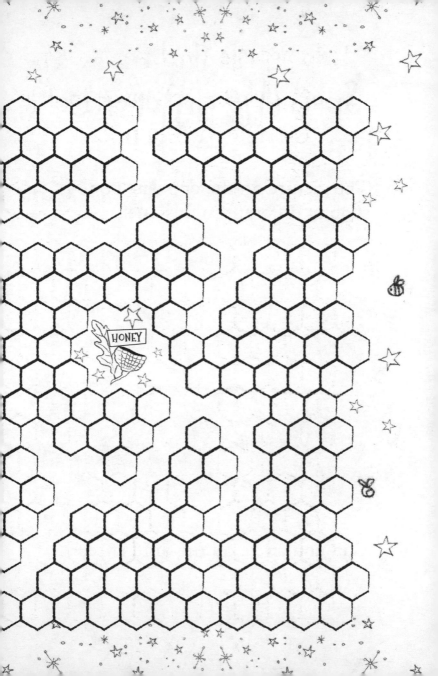

Spot the difference!

The picture on the opposite page is slightly different to this one.

Can you circle all the differences?

Hint: there are
10 differences
in this picture!

Fairy Animals

of misty Wood

Meet all the fairy animal friends!

Look out for
Daisy the Deer
and lots more
coming soon . . .

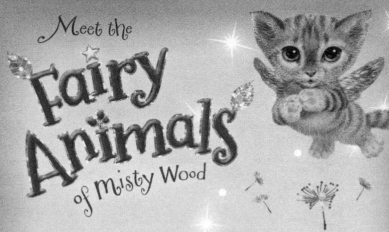

Meet the

Fairy Animals

of misty Wood

There's a whole world to explore!

Download the FREE *Fairy Animals* app and visit **fairyanimals.com** for lots of gorgeous goodies . . .

- ✳ Free stuff
- ✳ Games
- ✳ Write to your favourite characters
- ✳ Step inside Misty Wood
- ✳ Send us your cute pet pictures
- ✳ Make your own fairy wings!